Mike
has
Chicken-pox

A DOCTOR SPOT CASE BOOK

For Duncan

First published in the UK in 2002 by
Red Kite Books, an imprint of Haldane Mason Ltd
59 Chepstow Road, London W2 5BP
e-mail: haldane.mason@dial.pipex.com

ISBN 1-902463-38-2

A HALDANE MASON BOOK

Colour reproduction by CK Digital Ltd, UK

Printed in the UAE

Please note:
The information presented in this book is intended as a support to
professional advice and care. It is not a substitute for medical diagnosis or
treatment. Always consult your doctor if your child is ill.

"The Patients Association recognize the need for literature on children's
health that is educational and enjoyable for both the child and parent.
We welcome the publication of this Dr Spot Case Book."

Mike
has
Chicken-pox

Jenny Leigh

Illustrated by Woody Fox

ReD
KiTE

Name: Michael Monkey

Age: 5

Sex: Boy

Case Notes: Mike was a cheeky, lively young monkey who was brought to me covered in terribly itchy spots. Aha! I thought straight away. Chicken-pox! He wasn't allowed to go back to school until his spots had cleared up. What a lot of trouble his parents had trying to keep him in their tree house until he was better!

Doctor R Spot

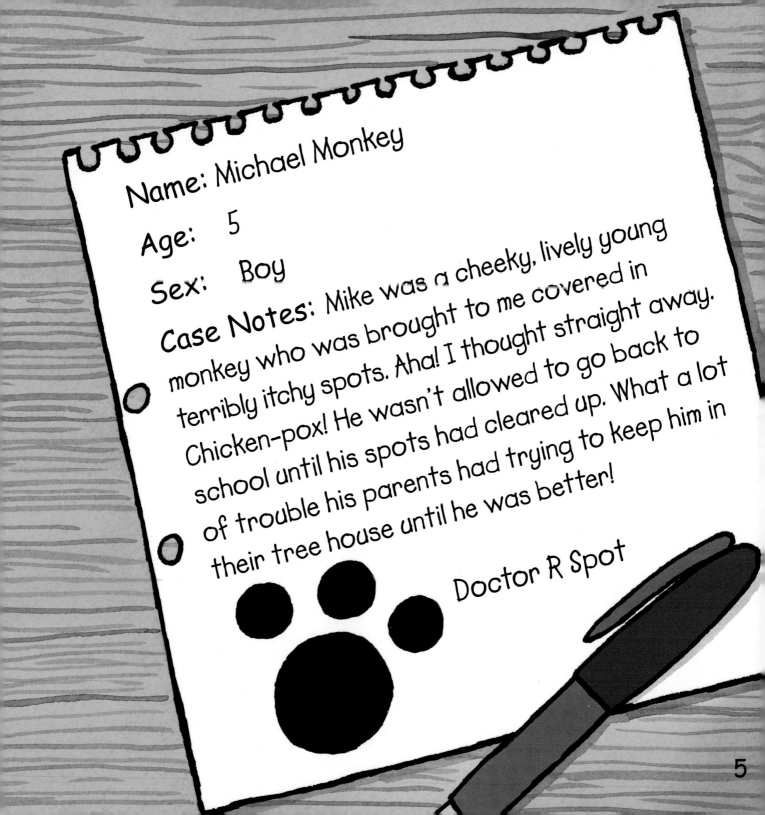

Mike was in a bad mood. He was playing tag with
Harriet Hippopotamus and Charlie Cheetah.

Harriet was so slow that she couldn't catch anyone.
Charlie was much too fast – he rushed and raced right
out of sight. Mike could climb up the tallest trees but
Harriet and Charlie were stuck on the ground below.

Oh dear, no one was having much fun.

"I don't want to play any more," said Mike. "Harriet, you're too slow. It's boring playing with you." Harriet started to cry.

"What a bawling baby!" said Mike, crossly. He flopped down against a tree and started to scratch his furry brown tummy. "And now I'm all hot and itchy," he wailed.

"Harriet might be slower than you," said Charlie, "but she's a great swimmer! And she can hold her breath for ever such a long time!"

"I think you're really mean, Mike," continued Charlie. "How do you think we feel when you climb trees? We can't follow you up there."

"That's because you're just a silly spotty cheetah. Spots here, spots there – you've got spots everywhere!" teased Mike. He laughed and danced about, pointing at Charlie's spotty coat.

Suddenly, Mike noticed Charlie staring at him. Charlie's eyes seemed to be getting larger and larger. He had stopped looking cross and was starting to smile. It was a very big smile.

"I may have silly spots – but so do you now!" said Charlie.

"Monkeys don't have spots, everyone knows that!" said Mike, matter-of-factly.

"Well, you do," said Charlie. "And they must be itchy – you've been scratching all morning."

13

"Tell him to stop it, Harriet," sulked Mike. "He's making me feel all itchy!" Harriet walked over and took a close look at her friend.

"He's right, Mike, you are all spotty!" said Harriet as she tried hard not to smile.

"I think you're both really mean," wailed Mike, and he scampered up the nearest tree and swung home across the treetops.

"Mu-u-um," wailed Mike, "Harriet and Charlie are being horrible to me."

Mrs Monkey turned round, gasped and dropped the bananas she was holding.

"Oh my goodness!" she cried. "You're covered in spots!"

Mike burst into tears – big, salty tears that ran down his spotty face. But Mrs Monkey didn't call him a cry baby. She gave him a big cuddle and telephoned Doctor Spot straight away. He asked her to bring Mike in to see him after the other patients had gone home.

Mrs Monkey carried Mike on her back as she climbed down their tree and set off for the surgery. Mike felt hot and tired and tearful. "I wish Doctor Spot could come and see me at home," he said.

"Well, leopards can climb a little," said Mrs Monkey, "but our tree house is far too high for him to reach."

It didn't take Doctor Spot long to diagnose the problem. "You have chicken-pox, Michael," he said.

"But I'm a monkey, not a chicken!" exclaimed Mike.

"You don't have to be a chicken to catch chicken-pox," smiled Doctor Spot. "Do your spots itch?"

"They itch like mad – I've been scratching all day!" said Mike. "Do your spots itch, Doctor Spot?" he asked cheekily, and immediately wished he hadn't. Doctor Spot just laughed.

"Are you going to give me some medicine to make me better?" asked Mike.

"Well, you will get better on your own in a week or so, but I will give you some lotion to help the itching," said Doctor Spot.

"Try not to scratch the spots, because it will make them much worse and they could leave scars," Doctor Spot told Mike. He looked quite stern and Mike promised that he would try very, very hard not to scratch them.

Doctor Spot told Mrs Monkey that Mike would have to stay at home for at least seven days, and that he wasn't allowed to see any of his friends during that time in case he gave them chicken-pox too! Mike didn't like staying at home and not being able to see his friends.

Mrs Monkey dabbed his spots with Doctor Spot's pink calamine lotion and brought him colouring books. Mr Monkey played games with him and read him stories, but poor Mike was very bored.

First his spots turned into blisters. Then the blisters popped and they turned all crusty. But Mike was really good and managed not to scratch his spots much at all.

"I don't feel ill any more, Mum," said Mike. "Can I go out to play with Harriet and Charlie?"

"Doctor Spot said that you had to wait until the crusty spots are gone," said Mrs Monkey. "Besides, I thought Harriet and Charlie were being mean to you."

Mike missed his friends and he felt rather guilty. He knew that he was the one who had been mean to them.

Slowly, the crusty spots fell off and, though he still
looked a little blotchy, Mike was allowed to go out and
play with his friends again.

"Hello, Mike!" called Charlie. "Still a bit spotty, then?"

"Yes," said Mike. "I'm sorry I was mean to you both. You have very nice spots, Charlie, not at all like the ones I had – they were horrid and itchy!"

"I'm sorry too," said Charlie. "We missed you."

"Let's play a game," said Harriet. "You choose, Mike."

"Anything," said Mike, "as long as it's not tag!"

Parents' pages: Chicken-pox

What are the symptoms?

- Slight temperature
- Runny nose, cough
- Loss of appetite
- Headache

These symptoms usually occur 24 to 48 hours before spots appear. Itchy, raised spots that blister and then scab over start on the chest, back or face, and spread to the whole body.

What should I do?

- Contact your doctor to confirm the diagnosis. Do not take your child to the doctor's surgery unless you are asked to, as the child will be infectious
- Keep your child away from school and elderly people
- Inform pregnant women who have been in contact with your child (pregnant women who have not had chicken-pox are at risk)

Will my doctor prescribe a medicine?

- Your doctor may prescribe an anti-infective cream if the spots become infected
- He may advise something to help your child sleep, or to lower their temperature

Doctor Spot says:

- Chicken-pox is spread by droplets from coughing and sneezing, and by direct contact with uncrusted spots. Children are contagious from about 2–3 days before a rash appears until all their spots are crusted
- Dab calamine lotion on spots to help the itching
- Bathe your child daily in baking-soda baths
- Keep your child away from school or playgroup for at least 7 days, or until the scabs have dropped off (they do not need to stay in bed)
- Trim your child's nails and discourage any scratching. Socks on their hands at night can help stop scratching while asleep
- Let the scabs fall off by themselves

Other titles in the series:

Harriet has Tonsillitis
ISBN: 1-902463-37-4

Poor Harriet the Hippopotamus has tonsillitis! Her head feels hot, her legs are all wobbly, her throat is very sore, and as for her tonsils, they are enormous! Luckily, Doctor Spot is able to help. He knows all about tonsillitis and Harriet soon feels much better.

Charlie has Asthma
ISBN: 1-902463-68-4

Charlie the Cheetah should be the fastest runner at school. But he's always running short of puff. Mrs Cheetah takes him to see Dr Spot. Dr Spot works out what's wrong and gives him something to help. Next time Charlie is in a race, he streaks around the track like greased lightning!

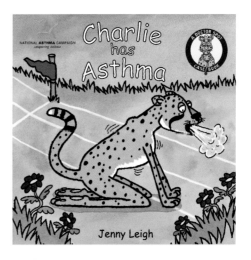